Cackle Cackle CROAK

by Rebecca Snay

To MS. Lockwood From Greyson

For Michael

Larry the crow loved singing. He sang
his heart out and then sang some more.

He thought his songs were divine.
He practiced one of his favorites
over and over.

caw caw

caw

caw

Larry's shrill shrieking went right into the ears of a little mouse. "Larry!" yelled the mouse. "My little ears can't take all this cawing!"

The mouse rubbed her soft ears and scurried away. Larry frowned, but this wasn't going to stop him from singing.

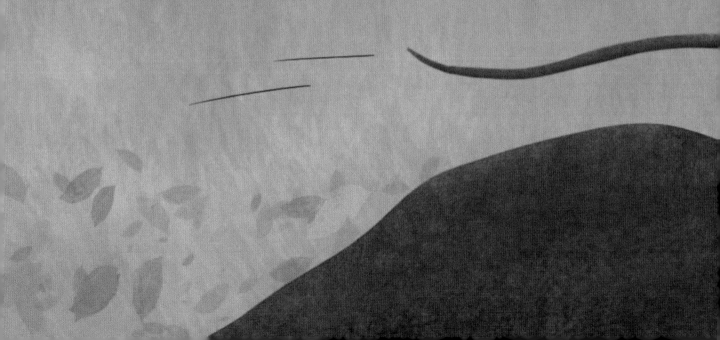

Larry decided to change his tune. He cleared his throat, thrust his neck forward, and belted out an old classic.

Squirrel was startled by the loud
noise and almost dropped her snack.
"Larrrry!" the squirrel hollered.
"Your singing is driving me nuts!"

Squirrel crunched her acorn angrily and scampered off. Larry plopped down on the branch, wondering why no one wanted to hear his singing.

Larry thought about what song would be a crowd-pleaser. He remembered a catchy tune from his childhood.

Deer was out for an afternoon walk. He was suddenly rattled by Larry's sounds.

"What is all this racket?" asked the deer. "Can't we have any peace and quiet around here?" The deer scowled at Larry and trotted off.

Larry didn't want to be all alone, but
no one seemed to enjoy his singing.
Larry sat silently and just...

listened.

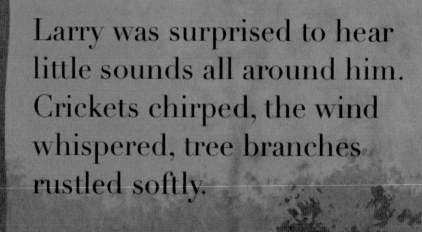

Larry was surprised to hear little sounds all around him. Crickets chirped, the wind whispered, tree branches rustled softly.

chirp
chirp

peep
peep
peep

Suddenly, a new song came to Larry. He soared up to a high branch and took a deep breath.

coo ♪

♪ *coo*

He pointed his beak skyward against the setting sun. As smooth as silk and as light as a feather, his song flew out.

All the animals fell asleep to Larry's sweet song.

With his heart warmed, Larry joined
them. His eyes closed and he dreamed
of beautiful melodies.

Made in the USA
Monee, IL
15 March 2021

62792594R00019